Quentin Blake

MRS. ARMITAGE
Queen of the Road

PEACHTREE
ATLANTA

To careful drivers on both sides of the road —Q.B.

Published by
PEACHTREE PUBLISHERS
1700 Chattahoochee Avenue
Atlanta, Georgia 30318

www.peachtree-online.com

First printed in Great Britain by Jonathan Cape,
an imprint of Random House Children's Books, in 2003

First United States edition published by Peachtree Publishers in 2003

First Edition
10 9 8 7 6 5 4 3 2 1

ISBN 1-56145-287-4

Library of Congress Cataloging-in-Publication Data

Blake, Quentin.
    Mrs. Armitage : Queen of the road / written and illustrated by Quentin
Blake.-- 1st ed.
        p. cm.
Summary: When the car her uncle gave her loses parts all over the road
Mrs. Armitage takes it in stride, but a gang of friendly motorcyclists
is impressed with the results.
    ISBN 1-56145-287-4
[1. Automobiles--Fiction. 2. Motorcyclists--Fiction.] I. Title.
    PZ7.B56 Mt 2003
    [E]--dc21
                                2003002113

PRINTED AND BOUND IN SINGAPORE

One morning, Mrs. Armitage came downstairs and found a letter on the doormat.

She read it to her faithful dog Breakspear. It said:

Dear Anastasia,

Because I am buying a new motorcycle,

I won't need my old car anymore. I would like

you to have it as a present. It's parked outside.

Here are the keys.

    With love,

    Your Uncle Cosmo

Mrs. Armitage and Breakspear went outside. There was the car.
"It doesn't look very exciting, Breakspear," said Mrs. Armitage.
"But we'll give it a try."
They climbed into the car, and off they went.

They hadn't gone far when they
drove over a big hole in the road:

bing   bong   dang   boing!

All the hubcaps fell off.

Mrs. Armitage got out to look at the damage.
"Hubcaps," she said. "Who needs them?"
She tossed them in the car, and on they went
to the junkyard.

But as they were going around the corner
by the vinegar factory:

> ## scrrunch!

The fender was ruined.

Mrs. Armitage got out to look at the damage.
"Fenders," she said. "Who needs them?"
She tossed them in the car, and on they went
to the junkyard.

They were backing out of the junkyard when:

skrrangg!

The front bumper caught on some old bedsprings.

Mrs. Armitage got out to look at the damage.
"Bumpers," she said. "Who needs them?"
She threw them on the scrap heap, and on they went.

They had just passed the supermarket
when a truck backed into the street:

skerrunch!

right into the hood.

Mrs. Armitage got out to look at the damage.
"The hood," she said. "Who needs it?"
She threw it in the trash, and on they went.

There was quite a traffic jam beside the new building site,
where a big crane was moving heavy blocks of concrete.
Back and forth it went,
        back and forth,
                up and down,
                        when suddenly—

kerrunch!

Mrs. Armitage got out, to look at the damage.
"A roof," she said. "Who needs it?"
She threw it in the trash, and on they went.

"Breakspear," said Mrs. Armitage, "I think it's time for us to get out of this town." They went down a side road into the country. All around them were trees, and the birds were singing.

"Breakspear," said Mrs. Armitage,
"this is blissful."

But the road got bumpier and bumpier:

beding bedong bedang bedoing

klunk!

All the doors fell off, and the trunk as well.

Mrs. Armitage got out to look at the damage.
"All this stuff, Breakspear," she said, "who needs it?
Let's throw it all in the trash, and be on our way."

But at that moment there was a roar.
It was Uncle Cosmo on his new bike.

His friends were there too—
Gizzy and Lulu, Ferdinando and Smudge.
They were out for a ride.

They all gathered round
to look at Mrs. Armitage's car.

"Wow!" said Gizzy. "That's a fantastic machine!"

"We're off to the Crazy Duck Café for a game of billiards and a can of banana fizz," said Uncle Cosmo.

"You must come too!"

"But first, have this leather jacket," Smudge said to Mrs. Armitage. "I've grown too big to wear it."

"And you and Breakspear must have collars," said Lulu. "I don't need three."

"And have one of our bendy flags," said
Gizzy. "We don't need both of them."

"And let me give you a horn," said Ferdinando.
"I don't need five of them, and it's always good
to have a horn."

Off they roared to the Crazy Duck Café.
And out in front, with her faithful dog
Breakspear, was…
Mrs. Armitage,
Queen of the Road.

E   Blake, Quentin.
BLA
           Mrs. Armitage.

$15.95   Preschool   08/11/200

DATE			

002986   9808445

Withdrawn

Little NEWTS

by Meish Goldish

Consultant: Dr. Kenneth L. Krysko
Senior Biological Scientist, Division of Herpetology
Florida Museum of Natural History, University of Florida

BEARPORT
PUBLISHING

New York, New York

Credits

Cover and Title Page, © Rene Krekels/Foto Natura/Minden Pictures, Jim Lopes/Shutterstock, and Milena Katzer/Shutterstock; TOC, © South12th Photography/Shutterstock; 4, © World History Archive/Alamy; 5, © Photononstop/SuperStock; 6T, © Kristine Hoffmann; 6B, © Pat Morris/Ardea; 7, © Photobank.kiev.ua/Shutterstock; 8T, © Pierson Hill; 8B, © John H. Malone/The Center for North American Herpetology; 9T, © Dwight Kuhn/Dwight Kuhn Photography; 9B, © Rene Krekels/Foto Natura/Minden Pictures; 10T, © John Devries/Photo Researchers Inc.; 10B, © Dinodia/omniphoto.com; 11T, © Gary Nafis; 11B, © Chris Mattison/Frank Lane Picture Agency/Corbis; 12T, © Solvin Zankl/Visuals Unlimited, Inc.; 12B, © Régis Cavignaux/Biosphoto/Peter Arnold Inc.; 13, © Warren Photographic; 14T, © Marevision/age fotostock/SuperStock; 14B, © age fotostock/SuperStock; 15T, © Byron Jorjorian/Photo Researchers Inc.; 15B, © age fotostock/SuperStock; 16T, © Andy Newman/Photoshot Holdings Ltd./Alamy; 16B, © Frank & Sabine Philippe Deschandol/Biosphoto/Peter Arnold Inc.; 17T, © Fabio Liverani/Nature Picture Library; 17B, © Joel Sartore/NGS Images; 18, © Rene Krekels/Foto Natura/Minden Pictures; 19, © Dwight Kuhn/Dwight Kuhn Photography; 20, © Gary Meszaros/Visuals Unlimited, Inc.; 21, © David Welling/Nature Picture Library; 22T, © Hugo Willocx/Wildlife Pictures/Biosphoto/Peter Arnold; 22B, © Henk Wallays.

Publisher: Kenn Goin
Editorial Director: Adam Siegel
Creative Director: Spencer Brinker
Design: Debrah Kaiser
Photo Researcher: Omni-Photo Communications, Inc.

Library of Congress Cataloging-in-Publication Data

Goldish, Meish.
  Little newts / by Meish Goldish.
     p. cm. — (Amphibiana)
  Includes bibliographical references and index.
  ISBN-13: 978-1-936087-38-9 (library binding)
  ISBN-10: 1-936087-38-3 (library binding)
  1. Newts—Juvenile literature. I. Title.
  QL668.C28G65 2010
  597.8'5—dc22

2009044166

For more information, write to Bearport Publishing Company, Inc., 101 Fifth Avenue, Suite 6R, New York, New York 10003. Printed in the United States of America in North Mankato, Minnesota.

122009
090309CGE

10 9 8 7 6 5 4 3 2 1

Contents

Eye of Newt

More than 400 years ago, English playwright William Shakespeare wrote a famous **tragedy** called *Macbeth*. In the play, three witches prepare a boiling, bubbling magic **brew** in a large pot. One of the ingredients they use is the eye of a newt.

△ In addition to the eye of a newt, the magic mixture that the witches in *Macbeth* make includes the toe of a frog and the tongue of a dog.

Newts are slippery little animals that are closely related to frogs and toads. Do they really have magical powers? Of course not—but they are shy, secretive creatures that live in unusual ways.

An Alpine newt

Newts are not very big. Most are from two to eight inches (5 to 20 cm) long.

A Double Life

Newts belong to a group of animals called **salamanders**, which belong to an even larger group of animals called **amphibians**. Frogs and toads are also amphibians.

The word *amphibian* means "double life." The animals in this group were given that name because most of them spend part of their lives in water and part on land.

◁ Most newts, such as this striped newt, split their time between water and land as adults.

△ Some kinds of newts, like this paddle tail newt, spend nearly all their adult life in water.

There are about 40 **species**, or kinds, of newts.

Newts live in water more than many other kinds of amphibians. As adults, they may spend less than half of each year on land. However, like all amphibians, they must keep their skin **moist**—even when they are on the ground. One way they do this is by staying out of the hot, drying sun. Another way is by producing a sticky **mucus** that covers their skin and keeps it from drying out.

Every newt is a kind of salamander and is closely related to animals such as this fire salamander.

Two Homes

Because newts lead a "double life," they have two kinds of homes, or **habitats**. Their watery home is usually in a pond or stream. Their home on land is in a **damp** forest or other wet, wooded area. During the day, they hide under logs, stones, or leaves to escape the hot sun. At night they come out to hunt.

The redbelly newt lives in cool streams and forests in California.

△ The black-spotted newt lives in Mexico and southern Texas.

Like all amphibians, newts are cold-blooded. That means that their body temperature rises or drops with the temperature of their surroundings.

In the freezing winter, newts **hibernate**. Those living on land keep warm under logs or in holes that they dig, called burrows. Those living in water bury themselves in the mud. The newts stay in their safe winter shelters until spring.

Eastern Newts in the Wild

Newts live in most parts of the world. These maps show where two kinds—the eastern newt and the Alpine newt—are found.

☐ **Where eastern newts live**

Alpine Newts in the Wild

■ **Where Alpine newts live**

Built for Land and Water

Most newts have small, thin bodies with long tails. In water, they wiggle their tails back and forth in order to swim. On land, they get around on their four legs, which are short but strong.

tail

adult newt

no tail

adult frog

Most amphibians are born with a tail. However, only newts and salamanders keep their tails as adults. In fact, scientists call newts and salamanders the "tailed amphibians."

Like all amphibians, newts can breathe through their skin whether they are on land or in water. They do so by using tiny holes in their skin called pores. The pores take in **oxygen** from the air or water around them. Newts also breathe in both kinds of places using the **lungs** inside their bodies. When they are on land, they use their lungs to take in oxygen from the air. When they are in water, they come up to the surface so that their lungs can take in air.

Even though newts need ▷
to keep their bodies moist,
they don't drink water.
Instead, they take in water
through their skin.

◁ Many kinds of newts, such
as this Japanese fire-bellied
newt, have colorful skin. They
can have areas of red, brown,
orange, green, or black.

Little Hunters

Newts may be tiny, yet they are able to get all the food they need by hunting. In the water, they swallow small fish and **tadpoles**. On land, they catch and eat small creatures such as insects, worms, spiders, snails, and slugs.

Newts
swallowing
worms

A newt is a tricky little hunter. Sometimes it sneaks up slowly on its **prey**. More often, however, it waits for prey to come close enough so that it can attack. Either way, the newt grabs its victim in the same way—it shoots out its sticky tongue and quickly pulls the meal into its mouth!

Newts have teeth to hold on to prey, but they don't use them to chew their food. Instead, they swallow their prey whole.

△ **This newt has just captured a fly.**

Staying Alive

When newts are hunting, they are also often in danger. That's because large birds, snakes, and frogs hunt and eat them. How do the little creatures stay safe from their enemies? Many newts, such as the red-spotted newt, have poison in the mucus on their skin. The poison makes the newt taste bad, so the enemy will often spit out the nasty meal right away.

◁ **This frog has captured a marbled newt.**

A snake ▷ swallowing a newt

Newts that have poisonous mucus often have red or other bright-colored markings. The bright colors help to protect them by acting as a warning to other animals. If an enemy attacks one of these newts, it remembers the animal's bright colors and bad taste. It learns to stay away the next time it sees one.

The bright colors of the red-spotted newt warn other animals that it is poisonous.

▽ A ribbed newt

The ribbed newt has an unusual way of fighting off enemies. It has needle-sharp tips on its ribs—which it can stick out through its skin and into its attacker.

Eggs and Babies

In the spring, male and female newts go to a pond or stream to **mate**. After mating, the female lays her eggs in the water. She may lay up to 400 eggs, but not all at once. In fact, some kinds of newts lay only two or three eggs a day.

eggs

A female great crested newt and her eggs

△ Newt eggs are covered in a sticky jelly.

Many kinds of animals, including fish, frogs, insects, and birds, eat newt eggs. To keep their eggs safe, some kinds of newts wrap each one in a leaf on a water plant. Other newts lay their eggs under rocks to keep them safe.

After about five weeks, the eggs hatch. The babies that come out are called **larvae**. They look more like little fish than little newts. The larvae have no legs, and they use their tails like **fins** when they swim. Also like fish, they cannot take in oxygen from air but instead take in oxygen from water using body parts called **gills**.

A smooth newt larva

After hatching, newt larvae breathe with their gills.

gills

Living as an Eft

Like all amphibians, growing newts go through a big change in which their bodies take on a different shape. Scientists call what happens **metamorphosis**, which means "a change in form." During metamorphosis, the gills of newts shrink, and they grow lungs for breathing. They also grow legs. When the gills are completely gone, the small creatures climb out of the water.

gills

△ **This great crested newt larva has grown legs, but it still has gills.**

A newt's metamorphosis is often different from that of most other amphibians, however. Instead of changing from a larva to an adult, many kinds of newts go through an in-between stage. During this time in their lives, the newts are known as **efts**. For the next two or three years they live on land, hunting for worms, insects, and slugs as they slowly grow bigger.

Most efts have rough, bumpy skin and are brightly colored.

This photo shows a red eft—which is what the eft of the eastern newt is called. Like all efts, it lives on land and looks more like a miniature adult than a larva.

All Grown Up

After two or three years, an eft becomes the size of an adult. Its body now goes through a second metamorphosis. Fins grow on the eft's tail. New organs grow inside its body so the animal can reproduce, or have young of its own.

△ This eastern newt was a red eft that grew into an adult. Like many kinds of newts, it spends most of its adult life in water.

No longer a larva or an eft, the little amphibian returns to a pond or stream as a fully grown newt. Once it is back in the water, its skin turns soft and smooth once again. Now built for a double kind of survival, the newt is able to breathe, move, and find food both in water and on land.

An adult California newt spends most of its time on land. However, like all other newts that live this way, it returns to the water when it is time for mating and laying eggs.

Newts can live up to 25 years.

Newts in Danger

Newts have been on Earth for millions of years. However, scientists fear that some species may now be in danger of becoming **extinct** due to diseases and changes in the **environment**.

Because newts take in air and water through their skin, they are especially sensitive to pollution. Also, as more ponds and streams are drained to make way for farmland and buildings, many newts lose their homes and places to mate.

In some places in the world, certain kinds of newts are already extinct. Here are two kinds of newts that are currently in danger:

Great Crested Newt

- This newt is found mostly in Europe.
- Great crested newts have lost many of their homes on land and in water due to construction by humans.
- Many of the newts have also died from poisonous chemicals used by farmers in surrounding areas.
- Today, it is against the law in England to kill or injure a great crested newt or to destroy its home. It is also illegal to own one as a pet.

Anderson's Crocodile Newt

- This newt is found in Japan.
- Anderson's crocodile newts are now dying out as people build new roads and put up buildings in the forests where the newts live.
- The newts are also in danger because they cannot get used to changes in their environment. If they fall into a construction ditch, they can't climb out and they eventually die.

Glossary

amphibians (am-FIB-ee-uhnz) animals that usually spend part of their lives in water and part on land

brew (BROO) a drink that is made by boiling its ingredients

damp (DAMP) slightly wet

efts (EFTS) young newts that live on land for several years before returning to the water as adults

environment (en-VYE-ruhn-muhnt) the area where an animal or plant lives, and all the things, such as weather, that affect that place

extinct (ek-STINGKT) when a kind of plant or animal has died out

fins (FINZ) the body parts of a water animal that are used for moving or steering in the water

gills (GILZ) the body parts of a water animal that are used for breathing

habitats (HAB-uh-*tats*) places in nature where animals are found

hibernate (HYE-bur-nayt) to spend the winter in a deep sleep

larvae (LAR-vee) baby newts after they hatch from eggs

lungs (LUHNGZ) the body parts of an animal or person that are used for breathing air

mate (MAYT) to come together to produce young

metamorphosis (*met*-uh-MOR-fuh-siss) a series of changes that amphibians and some other animals go through as they develop from eggs to adults

moist (MOYST) slightly wet

mucus (MYOO-kuhss) a sticky liquid made by the body

oxygen (OK-suh-juhn) a colorless gas found in the air and water

prey (PRAY) an animal that is hunted by other animals for food

salamanders (SAL-uh-*man*-durz) the group of amphibians to which all newts belong

species (SPEE-sheez) groups that animals are divided into, according to similar characteristics

tadpoles (TAD-pohlz) young toads or frogs before they become adults

tragedy (TRAJ-uh-dee) a play with an unhappy ending

Index

Bibliography

Bjorn, Byron. *Salamanders and Newts: A Complete Introduction.* Neptune City, NJ: T.F.H. Publications (1988).

Edmonds, Devin. *Newts and Salamanders.* Neptune City, NJ: T.F.H. Publications (2009).

Hofrichter, Robert. *Amphibians: The World of Frogs, Toads, Salamanders, and Newts.* Buffalo, NY: Firefly Books (2000).

Read More

Goldish, Meish. *Slimy Salamanders.* New York: Bearport (2010).

Morgan, Sally. *Amphibians.* Chicago: Raintree (2005).

Schulte, Mary. *Newts and Other Amphibians.* New York: Children's Press (2005).

Learn More Online

To learn more about newts, visit

www.bearportpublishing.com/Amphibiana

About the Author

Meish Goldish has written more than 200 books for children. He leads a double life in Brooklyn, New York, as an author and an animal lover.